"When do you visit that lot, Harry?" she quizzed. "You know that land is private property."

"I know who it belongs to," Harry said. "Mr. and Mrs. Jordan. My grandma is friends with them and delivers their orders for her cakes and cookies. I go sometimes after school and on weekends. The Jordans said it was okay for me to play there."

Mary cleared her throat. She knew Harry had conveniently left out the part where he sometimes went into the lot during school hours, too, to get lost kickballs or check out stinkhorn mushrooms.

The teacher wrote something down in her pocket notebook. "Well, I agree with you, Harry. That empty lot could be a great place for our science studies."

Books in the Horrible Harry series

HORRIBLE HARRY
and the Top-Secret Hideout

BY **SUZY KLINE**

PICTURES BY **AMY WUMMER**

PUFFIN BOOKS

PUFFIN BOOKS
An imprint of Penguin Random House LLC
375 Hudson Street
New York, New York 10014

First published in the United States of America by Viking,
an imprint of Penguin Random House LLC, 2015
Published by Puffin Books, an imprint of
Penguin Random House LLC, 2016

THE LIBRARY OF CONGRESS HAS CATALOGED THE VIKING EDITION AS
FOLLOWS:
Kline, Suzy. Horrible Harry and the top-secret hideout / by Suzy Kline ;
illustrations by Amy Wummer.
pages cm. — (Horrible Harry ; 33)
Summary: "When his best friend Doug discovers his top-secret hideout,
Harry enlists his friends' help to save it from being developed into
an apartment building"—Provided by publisher.
ISBN 978-0-451-47329-5 (hardback)
[1. Natural areas—Fiction. 2. Hiding places—Fiction.
3. Schools—Fiction. 4. Behavior—Fiction.]
I. Title.
PZ7.K6797Hnsk 2015
[Fic]—dc23
2015000658

Puffin Books ISBN 9780147515100

Printed in the United States of America

1 3 5 7 9 10 8 6 4 2

DEDICATED TO
the boys and girls at Castlewood School in
Bellerose, Queens, New York, for inspiring
this story. Thank you, Tamara Restrepo, the
teacher who asked me to come to Castlewood
for an Authors for Earth Day visit, and
Dolores Quinn, principal, for encouraging
the students to care about all living things on
our planet, including the nature preserve next
door, Queens County Farm Museum.

Special appreciation to . . .

my granddaughter Kenna for her interest in this manuscript and love of writing; my daughter, Emily, for arranging all my wonderful school visits; my copyeditor, Krista Ahlberg, for her very helpful queries; my husband, Rufus, for his many readings; and especially my hardworking editor, Leila Sales, for her valuable criticism, questions, and suggestions.

HORRIBLE HARRY
and the Top-Secret Hideout

Contents

Harry's Hideout

I never knew Harry had a hideout.

It came as a complete surprise.

He didn't tell anyone, not even me—
and I'm Doug, his best friend in the
third grade!

I finally found out about it one morning in May, when we were playing
kickball before school.

"Roll it fast with a little bounce,
Dougo!" Harry demanded.

"Okay," I answered, sending my best pitch his way.

Harry was waiting at the plate. *Bam!* He kicked the swirling red ball hard. It went zooming into the air high above Song Lee in left field. After it hit the ground and bounced four times, it rolled through the one hole in our school fence!

Everyone groaned.

"Game over!" Mary snapped.

"Oh, Harry!" Sidney complained.

As Harry rounded the bases, Song Lee and I curled our fingers through the chain-link fence. The ball had landed by the oak tree in the empty lot.

Harry jumped into the air when he landed on home plate. *"Home run!"* he screamed.

His team wasn't cheering. Dexter plopped down on the playground. "Game over," he repeated.

Harry stopped cheering. "No problem, guys. I'll get it!"

"Harry Spooger!" Mary objected. "There is a *fence* around that empty lot for a reason. It's private property!

You're not supposed to go in there. Look, the yard teacher is standing over by the steps. She'll see you go through the hole!"

"No, she won't!" Harry exclaimed. He rushed over to Song Lee and me. "Okay, guys, I need you to make a human wall."

Song Lee and I rolled our eyes. We had done that once before, when Harry had gone into the lot to look at stink-horn mushrooms.

Song Lee and I slowly stepped together till we were side by side. Our backs were two feet from the fence. We were standing so close, a fly couldn't get between us. Harry rattled the fence as he crawled through the hole into the lot.

"Don't move," I whispered.

"I won't," Song Lee replied.

Just as Harry reappeared with the ball, Mary, Ida, and Sidney came over and joined us.

"Harry!" Mary scolded. "I told you *not* to go in that lot!"

Harry flashed a toothy grin. "Look, Mare! I saved our custodian, Mr. Beausoleil, some work. He shouldn't have to find stuff for us. Now we can continue our game." Harry tossed the ball to Mary.

She exhaled loudly as she caught it. Then she ran back to the kickball diamond with Sid and Ida, screaming, *"I'm up!"*

Song Lee chuckled.

Harry and I shook our heads.

Mary! I thought, stepping away.

"Hang on, Doug," Harry said. "I have to check on something. When I was in the lot, I noticed a new sign had been put up. It faces the street. I have to go back and read what it says."

Probably "No trespassing!" I thought.

Before we had a chance to object, Harry dropped to his knees and headed for the hole. We had to protect him! Quickly, Song Lee and I stepped together to make another human wall. Seconds later, the morning bell rang.

Everyone raced over to line up. Mr. Ollie, the fourth grade teacher, was standing at the red double doors at the entrance of the school, greeting everyone.

"Harry, hurry up!" I said.

"Mr. Ollie will see us here!" Song Lee added.

"You guys go on!" Harry yelled back. "I have to read that sign in front of the lot. I'll stay in my hideout until it's all clear."

"Hideout?" we both repeated. That was news!

Song Lee and I turned around to face the lot. Neither of us could see Harry. "Where are you?" I called.

"I'll sneak back in a few minutes. I've been tardy before. Go ahead!" Harry called out from somewhere.

"Well, we can't stand here," Song Lee said. "Let's go, Doug!"

So we ran to the end of Room 3B's line.

When we turned around, all we could see was the empty lot behind the fence.

Where was Harry's hideout?

Oh No!

I couldn't believe what followed in the classroom.

There we were, sitting in Room 3B, watching the South School TV station, when Mr. Cardini, the principal, appeared on the screen. "I have a very special announcement to make," he said. "Miss Mackle got married last weekend. She took her husband's last name, so you should now call her Mrs.

Flaubert. That's pronounced *flow-bear*! As a wedding gift to her, I am asking Mr. Beausoleil to repair the hole in our school fence this morning. It's been something she has wanted for several years now, so I think it's the perfect present. Have a great day, everyone!"

Our class cheered, except Song Lee and me. We knew it was bad news for Harry! I was worried the custodian would repair the hole before Harry had a chance to make it back through.

"Finally!" the teacher exclaimed, turning off the TV. "Now we'll have fewer lost balls."

Mary looked around. "Hey, where's Harry?" she asked. "We were just playing kickball together outside."

Miss Mackle looked at me. (I know

her name isn't that anymore, but it's what I was still thinking in my brain.) "Doug, do you know where Harry is?"

"Ah . . . in the bathroom," I fibbed. "He'll be here soon." I immediately got up to sharpen my pencil. I didn't feel good about lying.

When I looked out the open window, I could see the playground and the empty lot beyond the fence. I stood there as long as I could, just staring at the tall grass, bushes, and trees. I was hoping to spot Harry.

Yes! There he was, crawling toward the fence! Just as he was about to duck down and go through the hole, I saw Mr. Beausoleil wheeling a barrow of tools and new chain links across the playground. He was headed for the same place Harry was! Harry couldn't miss him. The rickety wheel was making a loud noise.

"Doug!" the teacher called out. "Please join our circle for morning conversation."

Oh no! Harry would be caught sneaking out of school and trespassing on private property for sure!

As I sat down on the yellow moon rug, I had horrible thoughts about Harry being caught. Would he be suspended? Or would Mr. Beausoleil let him off because Harry helps him clean up after spaghetti day in the cafeteria?

When I snapped back to the present, Sidney was talking about his weekend in New York City. "Saturday night, Mom and I got to go with my stepdad to his convention! The best part was the four-star hotel we stayed in. You should see all the free stuff I got!" He pulled out a shower cap and put it on his head.

"It fits perfectly, Sidney," the teacher replied. Then she looked over at me and whispered, "Doug, would you check on Harry in the boys' bathroom?"

"Sure." I jumped up.

As I hustled toward the door, Song

Lee shot me a look. I had the same desperate feeling.

This was crunch time! When I got to the stairway, I began thinking . . . *What* was I going to say to Miss Mackle when I got back?

I stepped into the boys' bathroom and started pumping the soap dispenser. I needed more time to think. As I washed my hands, I glanced into the mirror.

Harry was standing there behind me!

I nearly jumped out of my skin. "You made it!" I said, turning around.

"I did," Harry replied, walking into a bathroom stall.

"But . . ." I gasped. "Didn't Mr. Beausoleil see you?"

"Nope."

"Wasn't he repairing the hole in the fence?"

"He was, so I went over it."

"You *climbed* over the school fence?" I said.

"Yup, down by the Dumpster, away from Mr. Beausoleil's view."

"Man, that was daring!" I exclaimed.

"Not really. The playground was empty." Harry groaned.

"How come you're so bummed?" I asked.

"I read the sign, Dougo." He flushed the toilet. When he opened the stall door, he had a long face. "It was a For Sale sign. I'm going to lose my hideout!"

"Oh, gee, Harry," I said, as he washed his hands. "I'm sorry about that."

We didn't say anything more going up the stairs. But I did notice something.

Harry had another problem.

There was a big hole in his jeans, and I could see his white underwear!

Oh no!

Pineapple Underwear

"Harry!" I called.

He didn't stop. He was deep in thought.

"You've got a hole in your pants!"

Harry skidded to a halt. "Where?"

"Your rear!"

Harry put a hand back there and felt the three-inch rip. "It was that chain-link fence. Can you see my underwear?" he asked.

"Yes." I groaned. "It's your white pair with pineapples on them."

"Oh, man!"

"I'll stick close behind you."

I was right on his heels all the way back to Room 3B. "Hey, Harry," I whispered. "Where is your hideout, anyway? And how come you didn't tell me about it?"

"I haven't told *anyone* about it!" Harry replied. "Just you and Song Lee today, but now . . . it's probably going to be knocked down by a bulldozer."

Harry sank into his seat quickly. I don't think anyone noticed his rip.

Everyone was getting their homework out.

"I have to mark you tardy, Harry," our teacher said firmly. "Next time, report to the classroom first, and *then* go to the bathroom."

Harry immediately sat up straighter. "I'm sorry, Mrs. Flaubert. It was kind of an emergency." Then he added, "I like saying your new name."

The teacher smiled. I had a feeling Harry wasn't going to get that tardy mark.

"I told you you'd get in trouble," Mary whispered to him.

He wasn't in trouble yet, I thought. But he was sure *sitting* on it!

The Empty Lot

The rest of the morning, we wrote about true adventures we'd had. Sidney's story had three pages on New York City.

Harry's was the best, though. He wrote about the empty lot next to our school. He didn't say anything about his hideout, but he listed some of the wildlife there in A to Z order.

Harry Spooger

A · corns
B · ird nests and beetles
C · reek
D · ragonflies
E · arwigs
F · ield crickets
G · rasshoppers and giant water bugs
H · umming birds
I · t is my favorite place to be.
J · dck-in-the-pulpits
K · atydids
L · izards and lightning bugs (at night)
M · onarch butterflies
N · ewts
O · ak tree and orb weavers
P · raying mantises and pill bugs
Q · uails
R · obins
S · aldmanders
T · ree frogs and toads
U · are missing a lot if you don't check out
                                    this lot!
V · isit this nature center!
W · oolly bear caterpillar moths and a woodpecker
X · tra stuff
Y · ou should go there!
Z · oo of life!

When Harry finished sharing his writing, the teacher smiled. "So you think the empty lot next to our school could be a nature center?"

"Absolutely!" he replied.

"When do you visit that lot, Harry?" she quizzed. Her eyebrows were lowered now. "You know that land is private property."

"I know who it belongs to," Harry said. "Mr. and Mrs. Jordan. They live in the green and white house next to the lot. My grandma is friends with them and delivers their orders for her cakes and cookies. I go sometimes after school and on weekends. The Jordans said it was okay for me to play there."

Mary cleared her throat. She knew Harry had conveniently left out the part where he sometimes went into the lot during school hours, too, to get lost kickballs or check out stinkhorn mushrooms.

"Mr. and Mrs. Jordan just put it up for sale," Harry added. "I saw the For Sale sign."

The teacher wrote something down in her pocket notebook. "Well, I agree with you, Harry. That empty lot could be a great place for our science studies."

Harry started rubbing his hands together, and I knew why. If the school bought the lot, then he could keep playing there!

"I did see some bleeding hearts and jack-in-the-pulpits blooming on the other side of the fence," Mary added. "I'd like to study wildflowers in that lot.

And draw pictures of them."

Song Lee joined the conversation. "Salamanders are beautiful. Have you ever seen any by the creek, Harry?"

"Yes! One crawled out from a hole in the ground near the water. It had yellow spots."

Mary shivered while Song Lee beamed.

"I wonder if there are any tadpoles in the creek," Ida said.

"There are lots now that it's spring!" Harry answered.

"I'll have a talk with Mr. Cardini," Mrs. Flaubert continued. "But no one should be playing in that lot without permission. Harry wisely goes there only when his grandma is visiting the owners."

Harry was tying his shoe so he could avoid the teacher's eyes. He knew that wasn't always the case. Like this morning, when he'd ripped his jeans going over the fence after checking out the sign.

There were two holes that had to be repaired that day.

The one in the fence was done. The second one was going to be a challenge.

The Hole Truth

When the lunch bell rang, I found out how Harry was going to cover that hole in his pants. He leaned over and whispered something to Song Lee. After she covered her mouth with her hand to keep from giggling, she handed him her sweater.

Harry tied it around his waist, and we all lined up. Everyone was so hungry, no one even noticed he had a girl's

sweater around him. It just looked white. Most of the flowers were on the sleeves knotted in front.

Dexter saw it, though, when he sat down next to Harry at our lunch table in the cafeteria. "How come you're wearing Song Lee's sweater? That's weird, man."

Mary, Sid, Ida, and ZuZu waited for Harry's answer.

"Because I have to cover up the hole in my pants," Harry replied. Then he chomped into his peanut butter and jelly sandwich.

"I ripped it on the fence," Harry added. "Right on my keester, as Grampa would say."

"Your butt!" Sid burst out. Then he cracked up.

Mary immediately objected. "I hate that word!"

"Maybe the nurse has a spare set of pants," ZuZu suggested.

"I don't want to make a big deal out of it," Harry replied. "I'll just use Song Lee's sweater." When he flashed a toothy smile her way, Song Lee giggled.

Suddenly, a voice came over the intercom.

"Boys and girls, this is your principal, Mr. Cardini. Mr. Beausoleil has just informed me that he found a piece of material on the top of the chain-link fence that surrounds our playground. It looks like it came from a pair of blue jeans. If anyone saw someone climbing over the fence, please see me. That's a dangerous thing to do. And we do not want that happening at South School!"

Song Lee and Ida covered their mouths with their hands.

Mary stopped eating. "Harry Spooger," she said. "I thought you got that rip because you went *through* the hole in the fence to get our lost kickball. I was okay with that. For one more time only. But you ripped your pants because you went *over* the fence! That's dangerous, and dumb! You could have broken your arm or leg! Someone could have seen you!"

"No one was on the playground. It was the only way back!" Harry explained. "Mr. Beausoleil was busy repairing that hole."

Mary stood up. "I'm telling Mr. Cardini right now!"

Deal or No Deal?

"*Wait!*" Harry cried. "I'll make you a deal."

Mary froze. She was still standing, but she was listening.

"If I promise never to go over the fence again, *and* show you my hideout after school, you don't tattle."

Mary slowly sat down. "You have a hideout? Where?"

"In the lot," Harry confided. "It's

really cool. I could take you there after school today. You could bring your sketchpad and draw wildflowers. Ida could see the tadpoles, and Song Lee, I'll show you where the yellow-spotted salamander is."

No one said no.

No one said yes.

But everybody was interested.

"We'd be withholding information," ZuZu said. "Mr. Cardini wants to know what happened."

"The principal doesn't want kids climbing over the fence. I'm not doing that anymore," Harry promised.

"I believe you," I said. I didn't want Harry to get in trouble.

"This seems like a one-sided bargain," Mary complained. "If we're giving

up *not telling*, what are *you* giving up, Harry?"

"My hideout. It's no longer a secret place if I show you."

"That is a lot to give up," Song Lee agreed.

"It is," Harry replied. "But you guys are like family."

Mary started eating her chicken salad again. "I'll think about it," she said.

"I'm in," I said.

"Me too," Song Lee, Ida, and Sidney responded.

"But what if that sweater slips off, and someone sees the hole in your pants?" Mary asked. "Then you'll be in trouble even if I *don't* tell on you."

Sydney snickered.

"I'd better sew up the rip in my pants," Harry agreed. "Do you have a needle and some thread, Mare?"

It wasn't an unreasonable question. Mary had more supplies in her desk and bag than anyone at South School. But she acted shocked. "Are you kidding? A sewing needle is sharp. It doesn't belong in school."

Sidney suddenly stopped snickering. "Wait a minute, guys. . . ." And he reached into his pocket.

We all watched him pull out that shower cap again.

"Sidney!" Harry groaned.

Then Sid pulled out a brownish-colored cloth for buffing shoes, and a plastic container with three Q-tips.

Mary made a face. "Would you please put your free hotel stuff away? It's grossing me out. I can't enjoy my chicken salad."

When Sid reached deep into his other pocket, he pulled out a very small sewing kit. Everyone stared at the three threaded needles in a small clear plastic pouch. One had white thread, another had black, and the third had pink. A miniature pair of silver scissors was also in the pouch.

"Yes!" Harry exclaimed. "That's just what I need. Sidney La Fleur, you're a lifesaver!"

Sid slid the tiny travel kit down to Harry. Harry grabbed it and gave Sid a high five.

"And I'll take the square piece of cloth, too," he added. "That will make a perfect patch to cover the hole!"

Sid slid the soft fabric to Harry.

"So who's going to sew the rip in your pants?" Mary asked. "Not me!"

Everyone looked at the other girls.

Harry stood up. "I am, of course," he said.

We all stared at Harry in disbelief.

"You know how to sew?" I asked.

"Of course I do," Harry answered. "Grandma taught me."

Harry disappeared to the bathroom for a few minutes. When he returned, he showed us his work. "Can I sew or what?" he bragged, turning around.

It was a horrible job, but at least you couldn't see his underwear anymore.

"Okay, guys," Harry said, sitting down at our table. "Are you with me or not?"

"I have two demands," Mary said. "You can't even *think* about going over that fence again, Harry Spooger. And Sid, you *have* to take that sewing kit home today. You aren't supposed to have sharp objects at school."

"I promise," Harry replied.

"Me too," Sid said.

"I believe you, Harry," ZuZu said. "I'm in."

"I'm cool with it," Dexter added.

Mary was the only one left.

While everyone waited for her decision, Sid took out a Q-tip and used it

to spread mustard on his boloney sandwich. "This free stuff can really come in handy!"

"Eweyee!" Mary groaned.

After everyone laughed, Mary added the last word.

"Okay, Harry," she said. "It's a deal."

After School

The plan was to meet at the school playground at three thirty. Everyone went home, changed into old clothes, told their parents where they were going, and met at the ramp.

Harry's grandma was there to meet us. Then she walked us over to the Jordans' house, introduced us, and sat with the elderly couple in their backyard. Just as we started to go through their back gate into the lot, Mr. Jordan turned to Harry's grandmother.

"I think I have a buyer already," he said.

Harry immediately stopped so he could listen. We did, too.

"Some real estate developer wants to put in a courtyard apartment complex. If I don't get any other offers, I'll have to sell it to them. Our retirement checks barely pay for things. But I'm glad the kids can enjoy the lot for a little while longer before that happens."

"I understand," Grandma Spooger replied. "That's why I have my kitchen bakery—to earn a little more money." When she looked over at Harry, she changed the subject. "You kids can play for an hour," she called out. "Just holler if you need us."

Oh, man! I thought. The lot was in danger of losing all of its wildlife. Salamanders and tadpoles would have no home in a big apartment building.

Harry shook his head. "There goes my hideout!"

As we continued through the gate, Ida, Mary, and Sidney hugged their sketchbooks.

Song Lee adjusted her camera strap.

Dexter lugged his guitar.

ZuZu carried a bucket and fishpond net.

As we followed Harry, we could hear a woodpecker hammering on a nearby tree. When a dragonfly flew in front of my face, I jumped.

"Don't you love it?" Harry asked. He made it seem like Christmas morning. I wasn't as crazy about some creepy-crawly things.

"Look, there goes a salamander!" Song Lee exclaimed. I took a step back while she snapped a picture. "Neato! Look at its yellow spots," she observed. Then the slimy thing burrowed back into the soft dirt by the water.

Mary sat down on a rock and started sketching a bleeding heart plant.

ZuZu caught some tadpoles in the creek and put them in his bucket. "You can see them up close now!" he hollered. Ida came over to look. As soon as Song Lee got a good picture, ZuZu poured them back into the creek.

After we'd had a chance to look around, I popped the big question. "Okay, Harry, where is your hideout?"

"We're very close now," he said. "Just follow me!"

The Hideout!

We followed Harry a little farther by the water, then turned right and walked toward the oak tree. "See the puffball mushrooms growing near the trunk?" Harry asked.

"They look like parachutes," I said.

He picked up an acorn cap, stuffed it in his pocket, and hoisted himself up onto the lower branch of the oak tree. "Welcome to my hideout!" Harry said.

Then he made a ladder-like climb up to the fourth limb and sat down on it. It was long and sturdy.

All of us looked up and clapped.

"Come and have some tree time, guys," Harry invited, swaying his feet.

"I thought you were afraid of heights," ZuZu said, setting his bucket and net down. One by one, we hoisted ourselves up and climbed to the thick branch just below Harry. Dexter waited and watched as he held on to his guitar.

"I am, but I'm working on it," Harry said. "Each month I climb a little higher. I'm up to eight feet now! Last month I could only make it to that third branch, the one you're all sitting on."

"How do you know it's eight feet?" ZuZu questioned.

"You'll see," Harry answered.

I positioned myself next to Harry on the fourth branch and dangled my feet. "I hate being afraid of heights," Harry continued. "It really bugs me. I thought if I could practice, I might get used to being up high. I feel good sitting here now. That wasn't the case last September, when I got the heebie-jeebies and goose pimples. I'm making progress. I didn't tell anyone because I

wanted to do this myself. But I'm telling you guys now, because I'm halfway to the top."

Dexter handed his guitar up to ZuZu, then climbed to the second branch. "Thanks," he said, taking it back when he was comfortable.

Harry pointed to a black box sitting on the thick limb beside him.

"What's that thing?" Dexter asked.

"My old mailbox. It keeps my supplies. I used some twine on either end and tied it to the branch."

"What kind of supplies?" I asked.

"Come and look," Harry said. Some of the others stood up on the tree limb, held on to a nearby branch, and looked straight up at the black box. Harry opened up the snug lid and pulled out

a handful of items. When he opened his hand, I could see what they were—the tops of acorns!

"Every time I climb the tree, I drop one in that mailbox. I have collected two dozen since the beginning of March." Then he dropped in today's acorn cap.

"Ohh!" Song Lee said with a big smile. "That's awesome, Harry!"

I could see how helpful it was to have a special tree for climbing.

"I also keep other stuff in there," Harry added. He took out a tape measure and pulled it out a bit.

When it snapped back into place,

ZuZu nodded. "So that's how you know how far up you are."

"Yup," Harry replied. Then he reached into the mailbox again and pulled out a big bag of gumballs. He gave three to each of us.

Everyone sat back down on a branch and looked out at the lot, the vacant schoolyard, and the long creek behind us.

"I like your hideout, Harry," I said.

"Me too," Dexter added. "It has a cool view. It's peaceful, too. Thanks for bringing us here."

Harry nodded. "I can't believe this place may be destroyed for a bunch of apartment houses. This is a piece of heaven!"

Song Lee snapped a picture. "It is," she agreed.

We just sat there for a while, chewing gum and dangling our legs. We listened to that woodpecker and to

Dexter strumming an old Elvis tune on his guitar.

Our peaceful thoughts were suddenly interrupted when we heard the red double doors of South School open and close. Two people were talking and heading for the fence.

"Look who's coming!" Ida shouted.

A Few Surprises

"That's Mr. Cardini and Miss Mackle!" Sid blurted out.

"Mrs. Flaubert!" Mary corrected. She and Harry were the only ones who didn't have trouble remembering our teacher's new name.

"Why are they coming over to the fence?" I asked.

"Mrs. Flaubert said she was going to talk to the principal about using this empty lot as a nature center," Harry explained. "They're probably checking it out."

"Who's in that tree?" Mr. Cardini boomed.

We climbed down and landed in the dirt. We met them over by the fence so they could see who we were.

"All eight of you!" our teacher exclaimed.

"This lot is a cool place," Harry said. "You should see the yellow-spotted salamander or hear the woodpecker."

Mr. Cardini was not going to be distracted by an amphibian or a bird. "You are on private property, kids. You should know that."

"Yes, sir," we answered.

"Do your parents know you're here?"

"We're here with my grandma," Harry explained. "She's visiting with Mr. and Mrs. Jordan next door. They said we could play here."

"All right, then," Mr. Cardini replied, immediately changing his tone of voice. "Glad you got permission. You did it the right way!"

Mary beamed. She liked getting praise from the principal.

At that moment, the Jordans and Grandma Spooger showed up. "Just checking on you kids," Harry's grandma said.

Mr. Cardini waved. So did our teacher.

Mrs. Jordan came closer. "I remember you," she said.

The principal smiled. "Mrs. Jordan! Mr. Jordan! Hello! It's been a long time."

"It sure has," Mr. Jordan answered. "I remember when you were just the same age as these kids. You used to like playing over here, too!"

Mr. Cardini looked a little embarrassed. "Yes, I guess I did play down by the creek a lot when I was growing up in this neighborhood."

"Did he always get permission to go into your lot?" Sidney asked.

"I caught him going over the fence once." Mr. Jordan chuckled. "But just once. His dad saw to that!"

Everyone looked at the principal and giggled. Then they looked at Harry. He was nodding.

Mr. Cardini's face turned red. "I'm happy to report I've changed my ways, Mr. Jordan. I don't climb over fences anymore!"

Everyone laughed.

"I see you're selling this lot," Mr. Cardini added.

"It's time. We need to make some improvements on the house, and the extra money would be helpful."

"Well, I'm hoping the city will make you a good offer, because South School is going to need more space next year for some portable classrooms."

Song Lee and Ida started jumping up and down. Selling the lot to our school definitely seemed better than selling it to someone who was going to put up a big new apartment building.

"But what would happen to all the plants and animals here?" Harry objected.

"We could preserve most of the lot as a nature center, especially by the creek.

We'd just use a little bit of the land for two portable classrooms."

Now all of us were jumping up and down.

"Make me a fair offer, and the lot is yours," Mr. Jordan replied.

"I'll see what I can do at the school board meeting!" the principal said.

"I'll be rooting for you," Grandma Spooger told Mr. Cardini.

Once the grown-ups said good-bye, Grandma Spooger reminded Harry, "You kids just have ten more minutes."

Harry groaned. "I know."

I tried to cheer up my buddy. "Your hideout is the best!"

"It sure is!" Song Lee agreed.

The rest of us nodded.

"Well," Harry replied, "let's hope the school can buy this lot so we can have it forever!"

Epilogue

Mr. Cardini and Mrs. Flaubert took the eight of us to the next school board meeting. Harry read his A to Z list, and Mary and Sidney shared their drawings of wildflowers. ZuZu and Ida reported on the life cycle of the frog. Dexter played a song with lyrics he made up about "Life in the Lot" while Song Lee's mom helped Song Lee show a slideshow. Everyone enjoyed her

pictures of the salamander, tadpoles, and woodpecker.

The board visited the property and decided it would be a perfect place for the two needed portable classrooms.

And they decided to make the rest of the land into a nature preserve for our science studies! Harry was kind of a hero because he got everyone at school talking about the living things right next door.

The best part was that *no one* ever had to go over the fence again. It was coming down!